AF575879

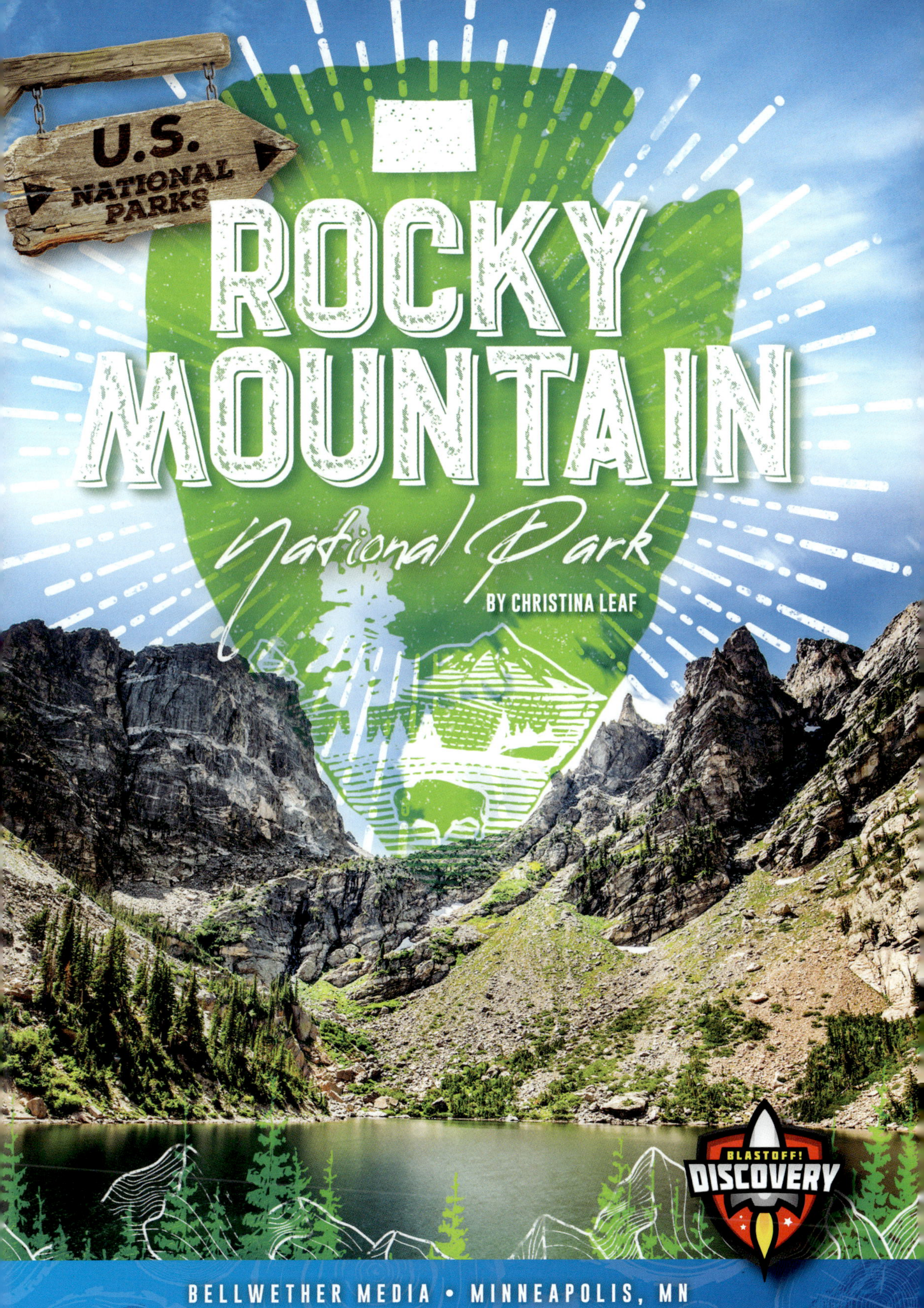

BELLWETHER MEDIA • MINNEAPOLIS, MN

This edition first published in 2023 by Bellwether Media, Inc.

Library of Congress Cataloging-in-Publication Data

Names: Leaf, Christina, author.
Title: Rocky Mountain National Park / by Christina Leaf.
Description: Minneapolis : Bellwether Media, 2023 | Series: Blastoff! Discovery: U.S. national parks | Includes bibliographical references and index. | Audience: Ages 7-13 | Audience: Grades 4-6 | Summary: "Engaging images accompany information about Rocky Mountain National Park. The combination of high-interest subject matter and narrative text is intended for students in grades 3 through 8"–Provided by publisher.
Identifiers: LCCN 2022016471 (print) | LCCN 2022016472 (ebook) | ISBN 9781644877555 (library binding) | ISBN 9781648348013 (ebook)
Subjects: LCSH: Rocky Mountain National Park (Colo.)–Juvenile literature.
Classification: LCC F782.R59 L395 2023 (print) | LCC F782.R59 (ebook) | DDC 978.8/69–dc23/eng/20220414
LC record available at https://lccn.loc.gov/2022016471
LC ebook record available at https://lccn.loc.gov/2022016472

Editor: Betsy Rathburn
Series Design: Jeffrey Kollock Book Designer: Laura Sowers

Printed in the United States of America, North Mankato, MN.

ROCKY MOUNTAIN NATIONAL PARK

ESTABLISHED IN 1915

EMERALD LAKE TRAIL

A family sets off on a hike along Emerald Lake Trail. They follow the trail through a thick pine forest before reaching Nymph Lake. The small lake is covered in lily pads. Beyond Nymph Lake, the trail skirts around Dream Lake. Ground squirrels leap across the path in front of the family.

A mountain stream rushes beside the trail as the family continues past Dream Lake. They spot a small waterfall tumbling off to the side. Soon, they reach Emerald Lake. Flattop Mountain rises in the distance. Tall peaks surround the lake's blue-green water. Welcome to Rocky Mountain National Park!

ROCKY MOUNTAIN NATIONAL PARK

Rocky Mountain National Park showcases the beautiful Rocky Mountains! Many people call it Rocky. It covers 415 square miles (1,075 square kilometers) of north-central Colorado. The town of Estes Park lies just east of Rocky. The town of Grand Lake lies to the west.

Rocky is in the Front Range of the Rocky Mountains. It is one of the highest national parks. Many of its peaks rise more than 12,000 feet (3,658 meters) above sea level. The tallest, Longs Peak, stands at 14,259 feet (4,346 meters) above sea level. The **Continental Divide** runs north to south through the park.

GRAND LAKE

ROCKY SEA NATIONAL PARK?

Around 100 million years ago, the area was covered in a shallow sea.

Rocky Mountain National Park began forming more than one billion years ago. Layers of **metamorphic** and **igneous** rock built up in the area. **Sedimentary** rocks such as limestone and sandstone later formed on top. The land was continually shaped by **uplift** and **erosion**. Around 70 million years ago, a major uplift began. The Rocky Mountains reached their current height about two million years ago.

Streams carved valleys into the rock. Later, **glaciers** moved through the area. They smoothed the valleys into U shapes. They also created narrow **ridges**, bowl-shaped **cirques**, and **moraines**. A few small glaciers remain in the park today.

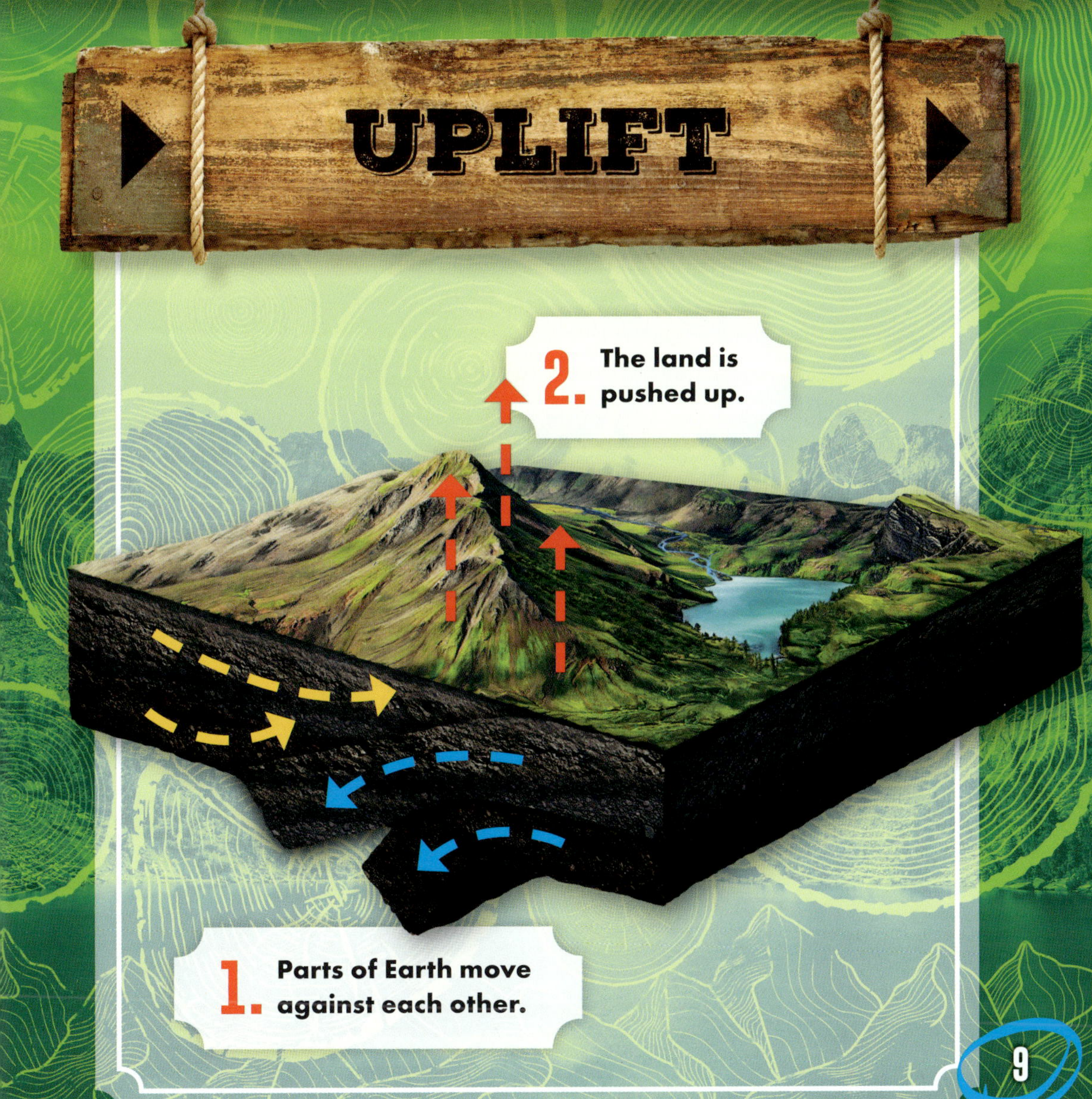

Rocky is filled with mountains, valleys, streams, and waterfalls. Evergreen forests cover much of the park. The **ecosystems** vary by **elevation**. Meadows, wetlands, and open forests make up the lowest level, known as the **montane**. Higher up, **subalpine** mountain slopes are blanketed with thick forests, while lakes hide between peaks. At the very highest elevations, treeless **alpine tundra** covers mountain peaks.

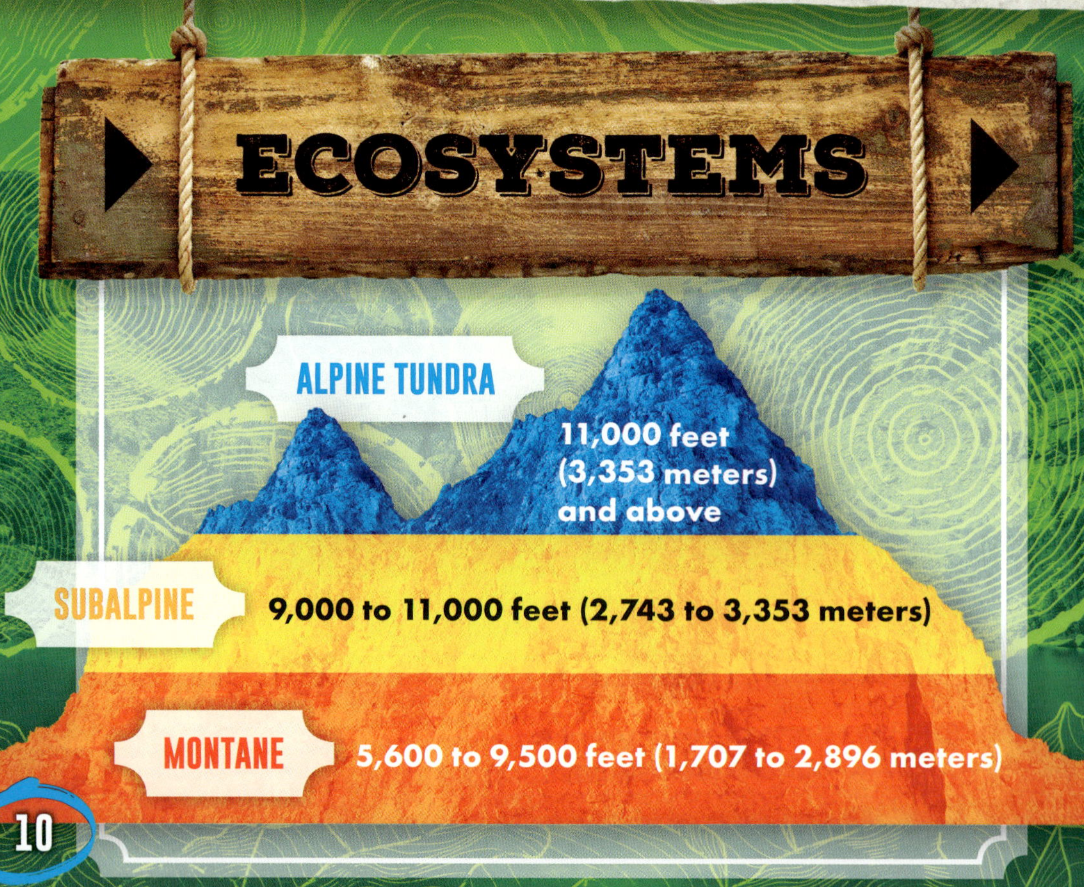

ECOSYSTEMS

ALPINE TUNDRA
11,000 feet (3,353 meters) and above

SUBALPINE
9,000 to 11,000 feet (2,743 to 3,353 meters)

MONTANE
5,600 to 9,500 feet (1,707 to 2,896 meters)

Rocky has four seasons. Winter is cold and snowy. Spring weather changes daily. Summer is warm, and thunderstorms usually occur in the afternoons. Fall is cool and sometimes brings snow. The western side of the Continental Divide gets more rain than the east.

PLANTS AND WILDLIFE

Rocky is filled with plants and animals! The montane zone boasts the largest variety of species. In its forests, ponderosa pines and quaking aspens shade the ground. Mountain bluebirds and western tanagers sing from their branches. Bighorn sheep scale steep slopes. Golden eagles soar overhead.

Moose search lakes for plants in the wetter western side of the park. Otters play in the park's rivers and streams. Badgers dig dens in open meadows. Wildflowers such as pasqueflowers, daisies, and irises bring color to the meadows. Western garter snakes slither through tall grasses.

BIGHORN SHEEP

ASPEN DAISIES

AMERICAN BADGER

MOOSE

WESTERN GARTER SNAKE

MOUNTAIN BLUEBIRD

Life Span: up to 10 years
Status: least concern

In subalpine zones, black bears lumber through the spruce and fir forests. Pine grosbeaks and mountain chickadees perch up high, while hairy woodpeckers drill into tree trunks. Mountain lions and coyotes prowl for snowshoe hares below. Wildflowers, including fairy slippers, twinflowers, and sneezeweed, dot mountain meadows.

TWISTED TREES

Trees called krummholz are found at the treeline. They grow more outward than upward. The wind shapes the trees into twisted forms as they try to survive. Some krummholz may be 1,000 years old!

Above the treeline, lichens and mosses cover the alpine tundra. Pikas chirp from their rock pile homes, while marmots soak up the sun. Forget-me-nots, alpine phlox, and other wildflowers lie low to the ground. Ptarmigans hide among small shrubs of willows. Elk munch on the willow leaves and stems. Many animals move between ecosystems in different seasons.

HUMANS IN ROCKY MOUNTAIN NATIONAL PARK

Humans first arrived in the area that is now Rocky Mountain National Park around 11,000 years ago. Little is known about these early peoples. Around 1,000 years ago, the Ute people began using the area as summer hunting grounds. They hunted for elk, bison, and other game in the area's meadows and valleys. They likely held an important Bear Dance ceremony there each spring.

BEAR DANCE CEREMONY

The Shoshone, friends of the Ute, were also known to hunt in the area. Around 1790, Arapaho people arrived. They challenged the Utes' control over the land, which led to fighting. The mountains provided a barrier between the tribes.

Spanish and French groups likely moved through the area in the 1600s and 1700s. In 1803, the land became part of the United States. Miners were drawn to Colorado in 1858 to look for gold and other valuable materials. When mining did not work out, some people worked as tour guides. As more people arrived, they pushed Native Americans out of the area and onto **reservations**.

In the late 1800s and early 1900s, people began trying to protect the area. In 1906, a group in Estes Park formed to protect the wildflowers and wildlife of the area.

MINERS

UTE TRAIL

NATIVE NAMES

In 1914, two Arapaho elders went on a camping trip with men from the Colorado Mountain Club. They shared names and stories about the area. Many Arapaho names are used in the park today.

Two people in particular helped the park become a reality. A man named Enos Mills fought hard for a national park in the Rocky Mountains. Mary Belle King Sherman fought for a park as well. She believed outdoor education was valuable for children. On January 26, 1915, President Woodrow Wilson signed the law creating Rocky Mountain National Park.

In the 1930s, government workers came to the park to create trails, restore the land, and make roads. Over the next 100 years, more land was added to Rocky. Today, it is one of the most visited national parks in the country!

OLD FALL RIVER ROAD

VISITING ROCKY MOUNTAIN NATIONAL PARK

Rocky is a hiker's dream! Visitors can take the 355 miles (571 kilometers) of trails to reach hidden lakes, gushing waterfalls, and tall peaks. People can also explore the park on horseback. Rock climbers scale mountain faces throughout the park. Anglers cast lines for trout in the park's waterways. Many people enjoy the park by driving along Trail Ridge Road.

TROUT FISHING

ROCK CLIMBING

TOP SITES

In winter, visitors can sled in the park's Hidden Valley. Ice climbers go up frozen waterfalls. Skiing and snowshoeing are other popular activities. Some people like to hike Rocky's snowy trails. There is plenty to do in all seasons!

PROTECTING THE PARK

Rocky faces several major threats. Harmful bark beetles are slowly killing Rocky's pines. Wildfires have become more frequent in recent years. Cheatgrass, an **invasive species**, is taking over areas where other plants once grew. This destroys the natural ecosystem.

Climate change is worsening these factors. Warming temperatures allow bark beetle populations to grow. They make higher elevations more suitable for cheatgrass. Warming temperatures also cause hot, dry conditions for wildfires. Cheatgrass and pines killed by bark beetles add fuel to these fires. The park's popularity also poses a threat. Too many visitors increases air pollution and puts a strain on the park's wildlife.

CHEATGRASS

ALPINE AT RISK

Climate change is shrinking the size of Rocky's tundra. Species such as pikas and marmots depend on this ecosystem. They will struggle to survive as temperatures rise.

Park staff are working hard to protect Rocky. Workers spray trees to prevent bark beetles. They remove trees affected by the beetles to reduce the risk of wildfires. They reuse the wood to improve the park.

Climate change is worsened by fuels such as coal and oil. The park has reduced its use of energy from these fuels. A shuttle along Bear Lake Road carries visitors to lessen car use in the park. Visitors can help, too. They can stay on trails and only make fires in allowed areas. Everyone can help keep Rocky wild!

ROCKY MOUNTAIN NATIONAL PARK FACTS

Area: 415 square miles (1,075 square kilometers)

Annual Visitors: 4,434,848 visitors in 2021

Area Rank: 26TH largest park

Population Rank: 5TH most visited park in 2021

Date Designated: January 26, 1915

Highest point: Longs Peak; 14,259 feet (4,346 meters)

TIMELINE

AROUND 1200
The Ute begin using the area

1803
The United States gains control of the land that will become Rocky Mountain National Park

1909
Enos Mills and others begin working toward creating a national park

WILLOW

JANUARY 26,
1915

President Woodrow Wilson signs the law creating Rocky Mountain National Park

1933–1942

Government workers build roads and trails within the park

GLOSSARY

alpine tundra—frozen, treeless land that is found high in mountains

cirques—steep-sided hollows on the sides of mountains that are often formed by glaciers

climate change—a human-caused change in Earth's weather due to warming temperatures

Continental Divide—a boundary on the North American continent that separates the water flowing east from the water flowing west

ecosystems—communities of living things that include plants, animals, and the environment around them

elevation—the height above sea level

erosion—the process by which rocks are worn away by wind, water, and ice

glaciers—massive sheets of ice that cover large areas of land

igneous—related to a type of rock that forms when melted rock inside the earth called magma cools

invasive species—plants or animals that are not originally from the area; invasive species often cause harm to their new environments.

metamorphic—related to a type of rock that forms from heat and pressure

montane—a mountain ecosystem at lower elevations that often has evergreen forests

moraines—areas of dirt and rocks that are left from glaciers

reservations—areas of land that are controlled by Native American groups

ridges—long, raised areas of land on the tops of mountains or hills

sedimentary—related to a type of rock that forms from layers of sediment that are pressed together; sediments are tiny pieces of rocks, minerals, and other natural materials.

subalpine—related to a mountain ecosystem that lies just below the treeline

uplift—the act of causing a mass of land to rise

TO LEARN MORE

AT THE LIBRARY

Lue, Julie Gillum. *What I Saw in Rocky Mountain: A Kid's Guide to the National Park*. Helena, Mont.: Riverbend Publishing, 2019.

Payne, Stefanie. *The National Parks: Discover All 62 Parks of the United States*. New York, N.Y.: DK Publishing, 2020.

Sommer, Nathan. *Colorado*. Minneapolis, Minn.: Bellwether Media, 2022.

ON THE WEB

FACTSURFER

Factsurfer.com gives you a safe, fun way to find more information.

1. Go to www.factsurfer.com.
2. Enter "Rocky Mountain National Park" into the search box and click 🔍.
3. Select your book cover to see a list of related content.

INDEX

The images in this book are reproduced through the courtesy of: Marcin Kopczynski, cover; NatalieJean, p. 3; haveseen, pp. 4 (Dream Lake), pp. 6-7; Margaret.Wiktor, pp. 4 (hikers), 27 (hikers); upungato, pp. 4-5; Markel Echaburu Bilbao, p. 7 (Grand Lake); Phanom Nuangchomphoo, pp. 8, 28-29, 30-31, 32; Sean Xu, pp. 10 (Chasm Falls), 23 (Bear Lake), 27 (shuttle bus); Melissa A. Woolf, p. 11; Paul Tessier, p. 12 (moose); Andrea Izzotti, p. 12 (bighorn sheep); pixel creator, p. 12 (aspen daisies); Holly Kuchera, p. 12 (American badger); Jeff March/ Alamy, p. 12 (western garter snake); Agami Photo Agency, p. 13; Nick Pecker, p. 14 (sneezeweed); emperorcosar, p. 14 (black bear); Richard Seeley, p. 15; Colin D. Young, pp. 16-17, 26-27; Transcendental Graphics / Getty Images, p. 17 (Bear Dance ceremony); North Wind Picture Archives/ Alamy, p. 18; Jim West/ Alamy, pp. 18-19; Everett Collection, p. 20 (President Woodrow Wilson); Kit Leong, p. 20 (Alberta Falls); SCOTT E NELSON, p. 21 (Old Fall River Road); Kris Wiktor, p. 21; P. Dorman, p. 22 (rock climbing); Bob Pool, p. 22 (trout fishing); Tobin Akehurst, p. 23 (Longs Peak); Claire Salvail Photos, p. 23 (LuLu City); Steve Bower, p. 23 (Trail Ridge Road); Joshua Boman, p. 24 (cheatgrass); David Spates, pp. 24-25; Robert Kneschke, p. 26 (bark beetle damage); Nikolas_profoto, p. 26 (bark beetles); Xasartha/ Wikipedia, p. 28 (around 1200); Erynmills/ Wikipedia, p. 28 (1909); Hoppyh, p. 29 (1915); Laurens Hoddenbagh, p. 29 (1933-1942); Ian Duffield, p. 29 (golden eagle); Holly S Cannon, p. 29 (coyote); Jim Cumming, p. 29 (snowshoe hare); Pam Walker, p. 29 (white tailed ptarmigan); Arina P Habich, p. 29 (aspen); Mykola Ivashchenko, p. 29 (pasqueflower); Pierre Ferreira, p. 29 (willow); Martin Mecnarowski, p. 31.